WAFFLES THE CHICKEN
LEARNS TO FLY

KEN AND ASHLEY MATTHEWS

To Hailey. Never be afraid to find your own way.

www.wafflesthechicken.com
email: info@wafflesthechicken.com
Rooster and Hen Publishing
Waffles the Chicken Learns to Fly
Copyright © 2020 by Ken Matthews
All rights reserved.
ISBN: 978-1-953352-01-9

Today was the day. It was GOING TO HAPPEN.

His outfit was perfect, fit for a hero! The grass was just fine, but he wanted the sky.

Waffles was GOING TO FLY.

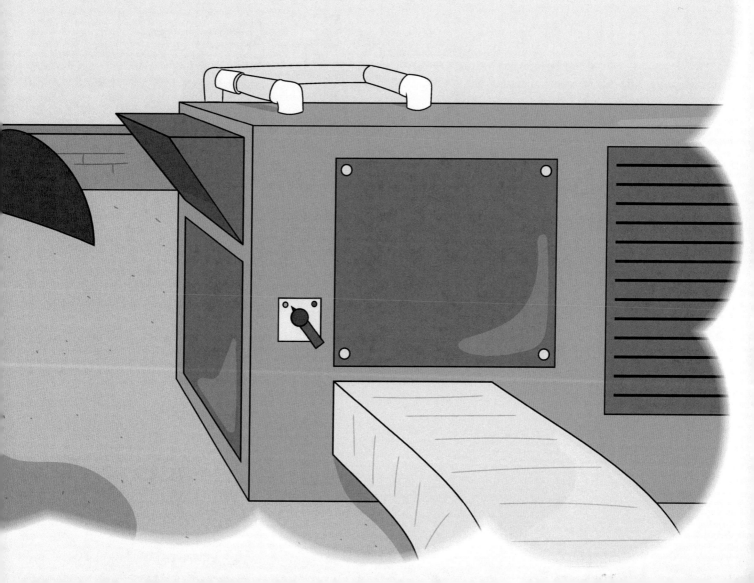

He snapped on his goggles, adjusted his cape, and climbed on his box.

... and fell in the grass.

"What a bad idea. Chickens can't fly," said dog.
"You should be happy to stay on the ground."

"No," Waffles said to himself. "I will fly! I just have to try! Next time I'll start closer to the sky."

So, he climbed on his coop.

From up on the coop, he saw the end of the farm. His friends looked like mice as they watched and cheered on.

He took a deep breath, he stretched out his wings, he took a big leap...

... and fell in the dirt.

“That was just dumb,” pig pointed and laughed.
“Chickens can’t fly. Don’t waste your time!”

"No!" Waffles cheered himself on. "I can fly! I will! I just have to try! Next time I'll start closer to the sky."

So, he climbed up the tallest tree on the farm.

From high in the tree, he saw a faraway town.
His friends looked like ants as they watched
and cheered on.

He took a deep breath, he stretched out his wings, he took a big leap...

... and fell in the mud.

"Wah!" Waffles cried and he sobbed.

His friends all ran off to go find his mom.

She picked him up quick and
took him right home.

She gave him a kiss and sat him down in the bath. Then she cleaned him all up.

"What's the matter, Waffles?"

"I'll never do it," he cried. "I try and I try, but I'll never fly. Dog was right. I should be happy to stay on the ground."

"It's true in a way," mom clucked and she cooed. "I don't know any chickens that fly."

"But you decide what you can do, not someone else. If you think you can, then maybe you can. Don't give up now. It's up to you to try."

"We are all so different. What works for someone else may not work for you. You need a new way. Try asking a friend for ideas."

"That's it!" Waffles shouted, and he ran out the door. He knew just what to do!

Made in the USA
Columbia, SC
07 December 2021

50634938R00020